Published By: The Daily Drunk/Shawn Berman

Cover Art: Canva

All Rights Reserved 2021 ©

Suggested listening music

The Daily Drunk Presents:

ONE ANTHOLOGY TO RULE THEM ALL

Edited By Josh Sippie

Foreword from the Editor, By: Josh Sippie	5
Lesser-Known Memoirs of Middle Earth, By: Lynn Hsu	7
Some think Tom Bombadil is God, but he seems more like a tech billionaire or a disgruntled, disinterested dad to me, By: Scott Cumming	8
Is it nice, my preciousss? Is it juicy? Is it scrumptiously crunchable?, By: Melissa Llanes Brownlee	10
Eowyn's Lament, By: Sara Dobbie	12
Concerning Hobbits, and Other Matters, By: Donald Carreira Ching	14
The Magician, By: Matt Schultz	16
Lesser-Known Memoirs of Middle Earth, By: Lynn Hsu	17
The Beatles' 1968 Tonight Show Interview to Promote Their Upcoming Lord of the Rings movie, By: Arie Kaplan	18
Sorry Peter, By: Charlie Walsh	23
I AM NO MAN, By: Miranda Powers	24
I can't carry it for you, but I can carry you, By: Shiksha Dheda	26
Lesser-Known Memoirs of Middle Earth, By: Lynn Hsu	28
The Dragon That Consumed Bilbo Comes For Me, By: Abram Valdez	29
Villanelle for the Blue Istari, By: Rick Hollon	30
Our Hobbit Hills Were Once Mordors, By: Andrew Sippie	31
Elevenses At Tiffany's, By Sean D. Zucker	33
Lesser-Known Memoirs of Middle Earth, By: Lynn Hsu	35

Watching The Two Towers with My Estranged Brother, By: Emma Mackenzie	**36**
A Quiet Pause in Another Place and Time, By: Jared Povanda	**38**
Lesser-Known Memoirs of Middle Earth, By: Lynn Hsu	**39**
Samwise Two-Times, By: Kip Knott	**40**
Grandma Got Run Over by Gandalf, By: Tanner Armatis	**41**
Fuck You, Tom Bombadil, By: Sadie Maskery	**42**
Sauron, my eye, By: Mike Hickman	**43**
Lesser-Known Memoirs of Middle Earth, By: Lynn Hsu	**44**
Look, I'm Not The Only One Who Wanted Frodo and Sam To Live Happily Ever After, By: David Calogero Centorbi	**45**
Thrice in Hand, By: Anna Fullmer	**47**
Final Pages, By: Rachel Bruce	**48**
River Anduin, near the Gladden Fields, By: Lauren Suchenski	**50**
Lesser-Known Memoirs of Middle Earth, By: Lynn Hsu	**52**
Contributors	**53**

Foreword from the Editor

By: Josh Sippie

You could call my relationship with Lord of the Rings… obsessive? That seems like the word for it. My wife and I rarely agree on what to watch and when we can't, we revert to watching Lord of the Rings. Usually the original trilogy, extended editions, because who doesn't love the awkward scene where Denethor hallucinates Boromir over Farmir's shoulder, but occasionally we will watch The Hobbit trilogy too. We hate Alfrid. Hate. No one wrote about that for the anthology, so I'm telling you, he's awful.

Lord of the Rings is *the* epic. It started everything. JRR Tolkien is far and away a genius of not just storytelling, but of creation. I mean, what writer out there can tell you the evolutionary history of plants in their fictional world? Who creates not one, but multiple authentic languages? No one does anymore. Not to this size.

Now, I'd argue that if Tolkien had access to Twitter, he'd have slacked a little. Maybe. But that's neither here nor there nor back again.

The point of this anthology is to celebrate our individual relationships with this incredible story, this breathtaking world (including but not limited to New Zealand), and these characters who broke barriers and built bonds we model our own characters and their relationships after. It's beautiful, damnit. Beautiful!

I should say at some point—why not here?—that Shawn did not ask me to do this anthology, I asked him if I could please, please, please do it. I was so curious what other people's relationships with Lord of the Rings looked like. Needless to say, I was not disappointed. After putting together this anthology, there are two characters you'll see more than any others. Eowyn and Samwise Gamgee. Eowyin, barred from fighting in the great war because she wasn't a man, to which she tells the world, "I am no man," before slaying the most fearsome foe on the battlefield. Samwise Gamgee, the true hero (don't even get me started on Frodo), who went from lowly gardener, a servant if you abide by the books, to carrying his best friend and closest companion the final stretch of the most perilous journey ever.

How awesome is that? In this incredible world, where Aragorn is invincible, Frodo is the "protagonist" (*rolls eyes*), Arwen is the queen, Legolas never suffers so much as a scratch, Boromir is the conflicted soldier who makes the ultimate sacrifice, Gandalf is benevolent and perfect, it's the characters like Eowyn and Samwise that captured our imaginations most. The characters who were consistently undervalued and doubted. I mean, Sam kills an orc with a frying pan. Eowyn kills the witchking and slays an oliphaunt while babysitting a hobbit.

That's another thing to love about what Tolkien created. It's not the heroes that win the story, though they certainly help. It's the regular people. The maiden and the gardener. That was the point all along. Your station doesn't matter, it's what you do with it. Which leads into my grand finale (can we call it that?) where I sign off with my favorite quote of all time, from our friendly neighborhood firecracker vendor Gandalf, and then I'll let the work take over.

> "All we have to decide is what to do with the time that is given us."
> ~Gandalf

Lesser-Known Memoirs of Middle Earth

By: Lynn Hsu

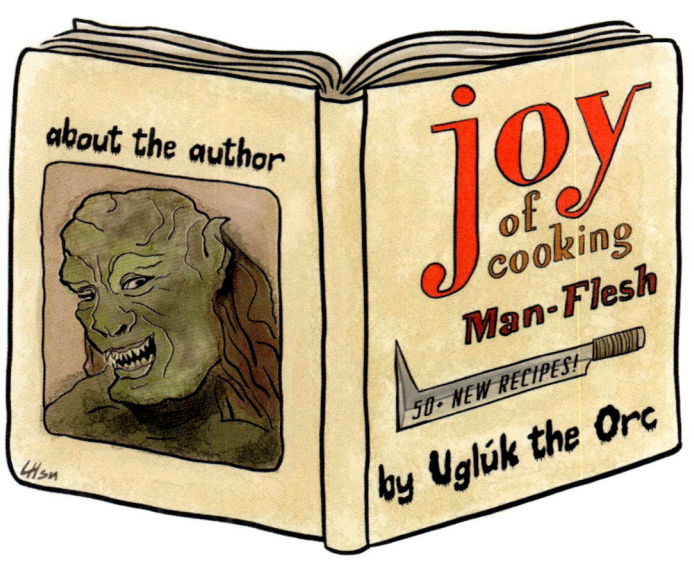

Some think Tom Bombadil is God, but he seems more like a tech billionaire or a disgruntled, disinterested dad to me

By: Scott Cumming

With every morning I opted for
another screening of The Two Towers
over class
My career prospects eroded
while the Gollum quotes cemented
until
We swears to serve the master
of any low paying job
that'll have us

Rock and pool is nice and cool
And so is punctuating nights out
with deep-throated shouts of
"Nazgul!"
and
"To Helm's Deep we must fly!"
as we trek between night clubs
a loosely assembled fellowship of the drink

From broken hearted tears
I could've formed my own Palantir
and found somebody more willing to talk
even with the chance they're hellbent
on the destruction of Middle Earth
it would still be more rewarding
than any more time with you

They kept Bombadil

Out of the films
but I'd say he's definitely
the most relatable character
as I drift into dystopian middle age
chilling on the sidelines of Twitter beefs
content
to while away days reading poetry
in the woods.

Is it nice, my preciousss? Is it juicy? Is it scrumptiously crunchable?

By: Melissa Llanes Brownlee

In a little fishing village there was a restaurant. Not a touristy, expensive, grungy restaurant, filled with visitors from the hotel down the road, nor yet an out of reach restaurant with nothing to offer price conscious locals: it was a pizza and sandwich restaurant and that meant delicious comfort.

Before I had ever read the books or even seen a movie, I had known of a special place called Tom Bombadil's. I learned the names of characters and locales from a menu, serving up Shadowfax pizza with sauerkraut and green olives, a turkey salad sandwich called the Hobbiton, and a marinara filled sausage sub, the Brandywine, my absolute favorite. I knew them all by heart. As we ate a pizza named Aragorn, meaty and cheesy, we would gaze up at a mural painted across the back wall with the whole of Middle Earth, and there in his forest, we'd see Tom. We'd wander through Rivendell, trace our way through Gondor, skirt around Mordor while sipping root beer and diving into our adventure for the day.

Sadly, Tom Bombadil's closed over twenty years ago, way before Peter Jackson revived a love for all things Tolkien again. Now, I am left with only a memory, but memory is not what the heart desires.

Eowyn's Lament

By: Sara Dobbie

How old were we that summer,
when we listened to
"The Battle of Evermore"
on repeat?

Fifteen,
maybe sixteen.

We'd close our eyes
as the opening strains
unfurled visions to us
of the Shire,
of the Misty Mountains,
of Rivendell.

You wanted to buy a mandolin,
so we searched
through every pawn shop in town,
you a hopeful minstrel,
I a besotted muse.

We bought a scratched copy
of Zeppelin IV on vinyl instead,
listening hard for obscure references
and mystical clues,
obsessed with Robert Plant's obsession,

and getting stoned
on your older brother's weed.

We holed up in your bedroom,
that portal to Middle Earth,
and you sang to me -
"in the darkest depths of Mordor,
I met a girl so fair,"
and you told me that Tolkien
was a Catholic,
but Jimmy Page
was a Satanist.

I figured I
must be a heathen,
intoxicated as I was
with High Fantasy,
with fantasies of you.

I dreamed of you
as Aragorn,
so when you told me,
the night before school started,
that you'd found your own Arwen,
working at the convenience store
on the corner of King street,

I became like Gollum;
a jealous, hateful creature,
hiding in dark places,
and mourning the loss
of some precious, precious thing.

Concerning Hobbits, and Other Matters

By: Donald Carreira Ching

Since he was ten years old, Devan has been a devoted Ringer, spending the last five years analyzing Tolkien's mythopeia and posting fanfiction on r/tolkienfans. TL;DR he's spent many a night arguing about the publication of *The Silmarillion*, writing verse from the perspective of Sam, and finding a fellowship to join him at Comic Con Honolulu. When Devan comes home with his eyeliner smeared over the purple polish of another black eye, his mother blames his father for helping him sew tunics and carving staffs out of driftwood. Then feels guilty and tells Devan, "Screw them and worry about yourself." He does worry about himself, so he tries on Boromir, Frodo, and Arwen. He logs on to his finsta account on Instagram, which he's not supposed to use because the last time something happened, he had to switch schools. Logan told his mom that they had kissed while rolling twenty-sided dice at Channa's. "He said you kissed him." Either way, the messages and comments didn't care what was true. Or that they all had done it. But he knows that the pull is not what they make it out to be. This is not the work of Sauron, or some Sunday school devil. He knows the difference between fantasy and reality. It is a ring forged and gifted to him, even if he hasn't figured out how he wants to wear it yet or what it means. So, on the morning of the con, he tightens the plastic armor he bought off of Etsy. He is Eowyn of Rohan. He is Legolas. He is the warrior he knows himself to be.

The Magician

By: Matt Schultz

Works on commission

Lesser-Known Memoirs of Middle Earth

By: Lynn Hsu

The Beatles' 1968 Tonight Show Interview to Promote Their Upcoming Lord of the Rings movie

By: Arie Kaplan

1968 was an important year for the Beatles. They had just announced their new movie production company Apple Films, which set up its first project, an adaptation of J.R.R. Tolkien's epic fantasy trilogy Lord of the Rings. So it's all the more tragic that we don't have a tape of their appearance on a 1968 episode of The Tonight Show, where they were hawking the movie. NBC's employees at the time didn't have the foresight to save the tapes, and entire seasons are lost to history. What does exist is the audio, recorded by a rather obsessed Beatles fan who captured the television interview by placing a tape recorder up close to their TV set.

Below is the transcribed text of the interview. Shortly after this talk show appearance, the Fab Four's Lord of the Rings film project fell apart. Therefore, this interview is all we have to go on, in order to try and envision the Beatles' proposed Lord of the Rings film. Consider it a tantalizing glimpse of what might have been.

JOHNNY CARSON: So tell us, for those who don't know, what is The Lord of the Rings about?

JOHN LENNON: What is anything about?

GEORGE HARRISON: That's the great existential question you should be asking.

PAUL MCCARTNEY: But to answer your question, Johnny, the Lord of the Rings books are about a thousand pages long.

RINGO STARR: Oh! I see what you did there, Paul!

JOHNNY CARSON: As do I. Look, fellas, just give us a basic rundown of the plot.

PAUL MCCARTNEY: It's about these four characters – hobnobs or whatever.

JOHN LENNON: I think they're called habits.

PAUL MCCARTNEY: Yes, habits. And the habits are going to toss this bit of jewelry in a volcano because their mum wants them to. I think that's why they do it, anyway.

RINGO STARR: Doesn't it have a unicorn in there somewhere?

PAUL MCCARTNEY: No, but wouldn't that have been lovely? A unicorn?

GEORGE HARRISON: Every book should have a unicorn.

JOHN LENNON: Unicorns are cheeky bastards. You can just tell.

JOHNNY CARSON (impatiently): So, your movie is about...

PAUL MCCARTNEY: Well, the books are about these four tossers getting rid of a ring or necklace or bracelet or something. Our movie's better.

JOHN LENNON: Yeah. In our movie, the four habits go to get rid of their earring or brooch or whatever it is, and on the way to the volcano, they bump into some girls. And the girls rip off our heroes' habit clothes, revealing to the audience that the four habits are in fact boyishly handsome international rock stars going incognito so as not to be recognized.

RINGO STARR: And beneath their shabby habit clothes, we see that they're dressed in foppish, psychedelically-inspired apparel what hurts your eyes to look at.

PAUL MCCARTNEY: The four lads are chased through the streets by a swarm of pretty girls, and this goes on for about ninety minutes.

RINGO STARR: The chase ends at the House of Lords, thereby justifying the "Lord" of the title.

JOHN LENNON: There's also some songs in the movie. New ones!

PAUL MCCARTNEY: Yeah. Well, they're really our old songs, with the word "dragon" substituted in a couple of places.

JOHN LENNON: Like, "I am the eggman, I am the walrus, koo koo ka dragon!" Or "Eleanor Rigby, wearing the face that she keeps in a jar by the dragon." Like that.

RINGO STARR: Also, "Love, Love Me Do" is now "Dragon, Dragon Me Dragon."

GEORGE HARRISON: We felt it would be wrong to just give our fans the same old, same old.

RINGO STARR: So these are new songs. Totally new.

JOHN LENNON: Almost totally new.

PAUL MCCARTNEY: In that they are now about dragons.

JOHN LENNON: Sort of, anyway.

GEORGE HARRISON: Dragons make a cameo appearance in the songs.

JOHN LENNON: They make their presence felt. As is the way with dragons, from what we understand.

JOHNNY CARSON: The next question on my cue cards is about how popular Lord of the Rings has become with college kids. But it's abundantly clear that none of you have actually read the books.

JOHN LENNON: That's true. But my assistant Gavin did read them.

PAUL MCCARTNEY: And he described them to us. They sound…very complicated. Everyone's this guy, son of that guy, who's the son of that other guy. "Aragorn, son of Arathorn, son of…" It's like the Bible. I feel like I'm back in bloody Sunday school!

JOHN LENNON: There's lots of sword-play in those books. Loads of stabbing. So much pronging people with bladed weapons. It's like, "Chaps, you're in the middle of a groovy fantasy world with elves and talking eagles and big floaty eyeballs. Can you not do violence on each other for like one minute?"

GEORGE HARRISON: I think if we were to do a totally faithful adaptation, we'd replace all the stabby-stabby bits with 11-minute sitar solos.

RINGO STARR: Yeah. Look, basically, I think the two things we'd want to keep from the books are the characters smoking pipe-weed, and…well, that's about it.

JOHNNY CARSON: Okay, so you are sort of kind of moderately more or less tangentially somewhat nominally familiar with the books…almost. Do any of you have a favorite character from the Lord of the Rings?

RINGO STARR: Yeah. Keith Richards.

JOHNNY CARSON: Excuse me?

JOHN LENNON: He means Gollum.

PAUL MCCARTNEY: There's also this one bastard, Gandalf, who's kind of like the Maharishi.

JOHN LENNON: But he doesn't act like the Maharishi.

GEORGE HARRISON: Maybe he isn't smoking enough pipe-weed.

JOHNNY CARSON: Fellas, before you go, any final thoughts about your movie?

PAUL MCCARTNEY: Well, it's still early days, yeah? I mean, we haven't even gotten permission from J.R.R. Tolkien yet.

JOHNNY CARSON: Wait, you mean to tell me that the author of the Lord of the Rings books hasn't even given you the go-ahead to make these movies?

JOHN LENNON: Nah. That geezer thinks we're just a bunch of scruffy-haired lunatics. But he'll come 'round soon enough. After all, like we say in our songs, "Love is all you need." Or as we'll be singing in these films, "Love is all you dragon."

Sorry Peter

By: Charlie Walsh

I stopped watching The Two Towers before the Battle of Helms Deep happened
yes I was that stupid
imagine right, getting up and walking out before the best bit of the whole film –
that was me
I did that
idiot

Remember "toss me"?
I don't,
left before it, mate,
remember that bit when Legolas goes down the stairs on a shield?
nothing,
weren't there,
remember that bit, right, when all hope is lost then out of nowhere Gandalf rocks up on Shadowfax with thousands of other blokes and flies down the hill to save the day?
zilch,
nowt,
nada

The worst thing is I love a good fight scene, me
the Airport scene in Civil War?
yes please
Rey and Kylo taking on Snoke and the boys in The Last Jedi?
banger mate
like, all of John Wick?
let's fucking go
so why, oh why, would I leave?
I honestly don't know

I AM NO MAN

By: Miranda Powers

In the darkness, hope I find
Loss when so young, tasting the brine.
I am no man.

Growing up tortured, looked over-still loved
Treated as pure as a white turtle dove.
I am no man.

Practice the blade, just for fun though
Not allowed to fight, so in secret I grow.
I am no man.

Hooves of horses, faces of strangers
Relaying to Rohan lifes lingering dangers,
We go...
To war...
But I must stay behind.
Doves cannot fight, only fly.
Fuck that- I go! In secret I must,
Sharing my steed with a hobbit of the shire.
So brave is that hobbit! Weening off my fears,
Separated on the battlefield, one day feels like years.

Crash.

My world shatters.

My King, my friend, the one I know as Father- but an uncle- is trapped under his steed with a Witch King and a Nazgul ready to give him a quick but brutal passing.

I run.
"I will kill you if you touch him"
"Do not come between a Nazgul and his prey"

I will be your prey first, but there is no need,
With my strength and my blade- oopss.. I just killed your steed.

Pick up a shield, stand tall but move quick
Avoid the metal spikes being whirled by this prick.

Hit and a shatter. My shield destroyed. My arm no good. I fall to the ground.

A hand firmly choking, my uncle watching in despair
"You fool, no man can kill me", as I feel my esophagus tear.

And one for the Shire! My hobbit friend is back!
Knifing the Witch King straight in his back.

As he hobbles over, I stand up tall
Grabbing my sword as I try not to fall.
I shove the blade in my enemy's face
As he starts to crumble standing in front of his fate
To hell you shall go, enjoy your little tumble.

Oh, and for the record..

"I AM NO MAN."

I can't carry it for you, but I can carry you

By: Shiksha Dheda

CW: allusion to depression, mental illness

but I am tired of doing that now.

We've walked through Middle Earth for years now
- you carrying the burden of your past, your thoughts, your misfortunes-
- me carrying

you.

Our small feet blistered from crossing fires;
hopping over foothills,
fighting off monsters
- cocooned in the web of moral dilemmas,

battling rough days,
crawling through simple days
- tough tasks make tough,
simple tasks made even tougher.

Forsaking calm green pastures,
you followed the ring,

I followed you

      –   both rendered homeless,
helpless.

The ring ruled us both
      –   planted mountains between us,
made us dance in the eye of tornados,
jump across oceans,

turned you against everyone
      –   against me,

you couldn't
wouldn't
see me
      –   see me struggle,
see me
try.

It's been years now,
the ring is gone

      –   somewhere -

far,

but its outline
still burns
my finger.

Lesser-Known Memoirs of Middle Earth

By: Lynn Hsu

The Dragon That Consumed Bilbo Comes For Me

By: Abram Valdez

Like butter that has been scraped with a dull knife
over too much bread, this year arrives uninvited.
My joints pull in winter and nurture the cold.
I do not remember this ache in this place,
or perhaps this ache birthed and nursed me.
I feel all thin; I feel all stretched; a lockpick
under the tongue for shackles that have long been
unchained. The story of my self which I tell
myself is a mare with no bit, a salve
of buzzard grease for scars I don't remember
saving. Truthfully, I avoid mirrors,
for fear they welcome strangers in my home.
If this is the end, why was I never told,
I could brave the goblins at the gate,
I could bear the fool in the tall grass,
I could burgle the affections of strangers,
yet my body would betray me before my heart?
Better for the journey to take me whole than to reach
the end under feet I never imagined
and with crooked fingers. How can the kiln
of a dragon's throat feel this cold?
What unsheathed this sting and seeded this decay?
I've earned the tankards to my health. You may have my eyes.
Do not mistake my wonder for surrender.

Villanelle for the Blue Istari

By: Rick Hollon

The great red book is wrong, is wrong, we hold
The men in songs forgot the wizards blue
For two they wore not swords but aprons bold

These two, they kept the bees, the herbs and mold
The hearth they swept and colic potions brewed
The great red book is wrong, is wrong, we hold

We halfling girls knew streams and glens of old
In secret studies gained the green way true
For two they wore not swords but aprons bold

In trees' dark roots the mushrooms vast unfold
From this we learned the loom, and woven grew—
The great red book is wrong, is wrong, we hold

The darkness kept at bay with honey gold
And midwife magic taught by wizards blue
For two they wore not swords but aprons bold

No battles brewed, no bloody deeds they sold
Istari came to aid our world, these two
The great red book is wrong, is wrong, we hold
For two they wore not swords but aprons bold

Our Hobbit Hills Were Once Mordors

By: Andrew Sippie

Sam, before the Fellowship, and I, before puberty, had no idea of the Mordors that awaited us. His biggest problems likely involved tending to the grass border beneath Frodo's window and gathering the courage to ask Rosie out. Mine involved lamenting my loss of free time that comes with more intense homework demands and waking up earlier for school.

One of my Mordors was making public speeches. As someone who wanted to hide away in mountain-fortress cities like Minas Tirith or write stories where I immersed myself in a hidden civilization living in a glacier, nothing could be worse. In high school, I was the student who sat in the back of class, ideally in the far corners, and never said anything or participated unless forced. I was happy to remain as invisible as Frodo while wearing the One Ring.

Despite my dread, when assigned to do a reading in high school speech class, I knew my topic: the words Sam spoke when carrying Frodo on his back through Mordor. As I spoke it in front of class, I felt Sam's courage. I realized he was not only carrying Frodo, but carrying himself because sometimes, we don't know how we can ever make the journeys we do, yet we still must take them. And others almost always help us along. Sam may have never been able to make that climb alone, and Frodo never would have. After the speech, I even received a compliment on it from someone I had a crush on. It felt like I had dropped the ring into Mount Doom myself. More importantly, I understood I could be brave, express myself openly, and not be alone in what I was feeling. Others listening to the speech seemed to feel what Sam and I did.

Our lives and struggles may not seem as significant as the massive battles for Minas Tirith or Helm's Deep. We may not feel as magnificent of a hero that Gandalf or Aragorn, but we still feel that dread and struggle, no matter where we are in life and what troubles we have. I am reminded of this when working with students coming from high school. Their deepest struggles of not having enough time for video games or hanging out with friends *and* homework may seem trivial to many of us, even if we've experienced them (I know I did). That's because life experience has helped us to know how to overcome our struggles. Sam likely felt it was much easier to ask Rosie to marry him after carrying Frodo to Mount Doom. Similarly, I find public speaking easier to face after having done it for years now, but it's still not easy.

Sam likely felt that every struggle he faced was the worst thing he could imagine, whether it was stepping out of Hobbiton, hiding from Nazgul, monitoring Gollum/Smeagul, walking into Mordor, facing Shelob, or carrying Frodo in Mordor. So do we. We may think it made the Scouring of the Shire, Sam becoming mayor, or his marrying Rosie easy. I don't think so. He likely still thought of himself as a gardener, just as I sometimes feel a bit like that kid hiding in the back of a class. We all have our self-doubts.

Still, what does change for me, for Sam, and I hope for all of us, is knowing we overcame the seemingly impossible. We may not have forged a city as majestic as Minas Tirith or faced a Balrog, but we can remember that we had the courage needed to do a task that felt as monumental. And when we remember, we can be certain that we will find the courage again since we've done it before, and especially because we're not alone. We've all felt our Mordors, but we can make them into Hobbit Hills.

Elevenses At Tiffany's

By Sean D. Zucker

She was a young socialite
Obsessed with fine jewelry
He was a writer
Comfortable and complacent

Also, he was a hobbit.

Their bond initiated when he moved into her building
Though a connection was far from assured
Or
From either's perspective
Expected

A food and drink loving shut-in
From a snug little hole in Bag End
An expensive escort
From upper east side Manhattan

Her promiscuous, carefree lifestyle puzzled him
His surprisingly large and exceedingly hairy feet
Made her hurl
Yet not look away.

Her closest friend
The upstairs neighbor, a Japanese photographer who
Actually
Let's not look too much into that.

She wanted nothing more
Than an older rich husband
He yearned for only peace and quiet
A comfortable place to finish his book

Following daily am trips to Tiffany's & Co
Might she of found the piece she was really looking for
In a three-foot-tall humanoid?

A classic tale of opposites attracting
But can they overcome their differences
Will cultural hurdles be ignored
To let love win

Is beauty truly in the eye of the beholder
Or is it of Sauron?

Lesser-Known Memoirs of Middle Earth

By: Lynn Hsu

Watching The Two Towers with My Estranged Brother

By: Emma Mackenzie

I like to tell people I don't know how long it has been since my elder brother and I last spoke, but it's a lie. I know down to the minute. Something I tell myself when I'm alone is that absolutely none of this is my fault. When I talk to other people about it though I pretend to take some of the blame, to make sure I seem self-effacing. On the other hand, he tells anyone who'll listen - shout out to our long suffering sister - that it's entirely and utterly my fault. Another lie I like to tell is I don't know why we became estranged, that it just sort of happened; like a random hobbit becoming the bearer of the one ring. But it had been in the works.

When we were teenagers I wasn't allowed to read the Lord of the Rings books until he finished them. Despite being highly intelligent, he wasn't a strong reader and I guess my mother worried that me racing through the trilogy before him would make him feel self conscious. This had been a theme of my young life: I taught myself to read before starting school (yes I'm bragging) because no one else would until he had learned to. Anyway, aged three and a half was when I made my first deposit in the resentment bank and learned a lesson that most women are all too familiar with: in this world it's important to pretend to know less than men so they don't feel bad about themselves. I was good to my word though: he never finished the books and so to this day I have never picked them up. Still, we watched the movies together five thousand times, so I reckon we got the gist.

It isn't like we could have one conversation that would magically fix things between us, but I really feel like sitting down and watching the Two Towers one more time would be our best shot. The first and most obvious reason for this is that we both know every word of the dialogue off by heart. So even if we weren't talking *to* each other, we'd be talking in each other's presence - which is basically the same thing, right? There is physically no possible way either of us can watch that movie without reciting our favourite lines, so at least some speech would be guaranteed. By the time we got to the "Po-tay-toes" scene part of us would basically be teenagers again, rolling our eyes at our friend's Gollum impression. If we watched the walls of Helm's Deep begin to be breached, we'd once more be giggling as we snuck our neighbour's cat into the house - part of a long term experiment we successfully conducted to prove our dad was lying about being allergic to cats. As Smeagol gave himself over to his darker impulses in the final scene we'd have reunited in the present day. I can see us now: reclining on the sofas and arguing about who's more annoying, Frodo or Sam, (it's absolutely Frodo) as we line up Return of the King.

The second reason this would be likely to work is that Treebeard is literally our grandfather. The resemblance is uncanny. Their voices, noses, the growths on their face - skin cancer is a nightmare, SPF 50 forever - and the way they think their existence is mostly separate from silly, human matters. On the drive home from the cinema we couldn't stop talking about it and how many times we, like Merry, had uttered things like: "But you're part of this world aren't you?" Only when we said it our grandfather would just smile and ask us what our names were again. He doesn't have dementia or anything, he's just self absorbed and decided retrospectively having a family was fundamentally a bit of a drag and he'd rather live on a boat. I feel confident that this reminder of a disappointing family member could bring us together. Maybe, after everything, we'd realise that it doesn't have to be my fault, or my brother's, that we fell out. There's a way we could lay this all at someone else's door and who better than the person who started this tidal wave of familial dysfunction in the first place? A person who might be occasionally sweet and amusing, but would never in any circumstances - not even deforestation - be persuaded to join us in the fight against evil wizards and orks.

All of this might not be enough to get over the decades of secret competition for parental attention, but if shouting across to him, "What do your elf eyes see?" doesn't at least produce an impressively committed "They're taking the hobbits to Isengard!" to break the silence, then I don't know what will.

A Quiet Pause in Another Place and Time

By: Jared Povanda

Uncurl your slender fingers from the bow's thin limb
and come into the woolen scratch
of my arms,
Legolas.
Let me hold you within the woodsmoke
and the falling embers from the cook fires
limning the swooping of your cheekbones
I wish I could take in my mouth
like bird bones to
suck the residual meat from the splinters.
"Aragorn," you'd groan, but then you'd smile for me, into that dimple,
because that's what we are,
Legolas.
Bone deep within the undulates
of the sensual body.
And will you share this shadowed dance?
Will you sway with me outside the circle
of companionable light?
The ring we'll make of our steps
will carry forth without flaw.

Lesser-Known Memoirs of Middle Earth

By: Lynn Hsu

Samwise Two-Times

By: Kip Knott

Everything I have to say, Mr. Frodo,
everything I have to say is so important
that I have to say it not once but twice.

Remember how I told you about Rosie,
Mr. Frodo? Remember how I said,
"If ever I was to marry someone,
it would've been her, it would have been her"?
Well it was her, Mr. Frodo. It was her.

And when I said, "Don't you let go.
Don't let go," as you dangled over the fires
of Mount Doom, I knew I had to say it twice
before you would take my hand.

And you took my hand, Mr. Frodo.
You took my hand and came back to me.
You came back to me, Mr. Frodo,
there at the end of all things,
as the one ring melted and set you free.

Grandma Got Run Over by Gandalf

By: Tanner Armatis

"Don't touch it, Tanner," Grandma was stern. Her voice insisting on the unknown. "It is the One."

Sealed inside the confines of a bowl painted with images of travelers, swordsmen, and wizards, it was there. The inscriptions, the gold, the allure to take it out and wear it. I couldn't believe she had it.

"You can only imagine what this ring can do."

"Have you ever used it?"

"I can't tell you what I did, but yes. I did a great many things." And she smiled, showing how she got her wrinkles, as she looked down at the bowl on the coffee table. "And I know what you're thinking. You're too young to wield this power. One day, when I'm gone, this will be yours. Now, c'mon. Sit with Grandma and let's finish this movie."

And as the movie played, Grandma held my tiny body under her arm and we cuddled in her brown blanket. But I didn't watch the movie, not only because I already saw it, but because it was no longer a movie with an ending. Mount Doom was no longer a grave. The women who held me was no longer just my grandma— she was an explorer— she was the succession. And her house decorated with her antique knickknacks was actually a museum displaying her treasures. The front room with her stuffed owls and birds were hunting trophies she caught on her adventure. The chateau red rug spread across the room was gifted to her from the King of Gondor. The wooden cuckoo clock was stolen out of a cave in the Blue Mountains run by Dwarves. Her white cat was a special breed of feline made from Elvish magic that caused her eyes to be blood-red and she was prone to lashing out against toes exposed underneath a blanket. And her life of impossibilities was possible because of this One Ring.

When the movie ended, I asked her, "Grandma, can you tell me how you got all of these things?"

And she grinned, remembering the times she told my young gullible mother they were eating snakes from Africa or crocodiles from Florida for dinner, and she sensed the curiosity brewing inside my young mind, the imagination amplifying from the possibilities of an innocent boy seeking an adventure.

And she said, "Yes, I'll tell you of my time in Middle-earth. It all started when an old man wasn't paying attention to where he was driving."

Fuck You, Tom Bombadil

By: Sadie Maskery

Who's merry and benevolent, who sits beneath the trees
And sings the tale of mead and vale, the butterflies and bees,
Who never cares if Saruman is closing for the kill?
There's neutral then there's negligent, then there's Tom Bombadil.

They failed to cross the mountains by the path of Caradhras,
And fought the Balrog in the mines (you bloody shall not pass).
They suffered hell to save the ring from Shelob's webby lair
And watched as Gondor's steward wept and set fire to his heir..
But while they fought and burned and died the earworm marked them still
As those who'd heard the folktunes of that bloody Bombadil.

You called your ponies stupid names whilst other righted wrongs.
The forests burned, the Entwives died, you sat and sang your songs.
So fuck off, Tom, you didn't hide the Bane of Isildur.
You let your friends set sail their ships beyond the western shore.
The willow tree, and barrow wights, those took a certain skill,
But that was all the help you gave, screw you, Tom Bombadil.

So when the battle's ended and the mumakils head home,
When Helms Deep is defended and the Gondor banners flown,
The white tree sprouting leaves again and hobbitses are fed,
The Ring a molten puddle and the Eye is truly dead,
We'll count the cost of all we've lost and send the final bill
To those who didn't give a toss. And you, Tom Bombadil.

Sauron, my eye

By: Mike Hickman

The thing with turning famous fantasy novels into blockbuster movie trilogies,

Is you run the risk of opening up your carefully crafted world to people who haven't lived orcs and hobbits their whole lives,

People who've paid their money, bought their popcorn, maybe added a *Rollover* hot dog or two to the order, if they're feeling flush, and have seen the running time.

People like the old lady behind me at the *Odeon* on opening night,

Who took one look at the mighty Eye of Sauron,

Torn by some gust of wind out of the world,

Manifesting itself within the swirling, mantling clouds,

Burning at the apex of Barad-dûr,

And wondered aloud,

In a beautifully timed and very rare moment of silence,

Precisely how rich you had to be if you had that thing on your gas bill.

Lesser-Known Memoirs of Middle Earth

By: Lynn Hsu

Look, I'm Not The Only One Who Wanted Frodo and Sam To Live Happily Ever After

By: David Calogero Centorbi

in some quaint, cozy, Hobbit-hole on the upper East Side of Hobbiton.
I mean, why was I in tears as they said their goodbyes on that hard boulder
surrounded by all that smokey, fiery, bubbling, lava?
Hell, I wanted to give them each other's goodbye kiss. They sure weren't
going to do it.

But okay, it's me. I'm the only one that read the *I Word* into their
relationship.
I Word?
Intimacy, my dear. What were you thinking I meant, Indecent?
Look, those two boys started off friends and ended up...
Here it comes...
LOVERS.

See, go ahead and give me your squinty-I'm-confused-you're-crazy look.
And yes, go ahead and argue it wasn't in the book,
and Jackson wasn't directing them with that intent.

And I will counter, I read the books like 20 years ago before I realized
two boys could fall in love with one another,
and who knows what was going on
with those two Hobbits after they heard, "Cut."
All I can really say is I know what I saw,
and I liked it even more than when Galadriel
strolled through the forest in her Ngila Dickson
designed, beaded Lady Of The Wood Gown.

But listen, the problem with this culture is it still cannot separate,

if you're not fucking, you can't be lovers.
Let me tell you. I had fuckers I knew could never be anyone's lover.
So, when you find the latter, who cares about the former—

you never know when the day will come
when Mount Doom blows its lid, and you'll be stuck on a smoldering
boulder surrounded by lava,

and you'll want to be with the only person in the world
you would ever want to say goodbye to.

Thrice in Hand

By: Anna Fullmer

I always held fast
that fanfic was for kids
like my 7th grade
Star Wars Adventures
written in a Lisa Frank
dolphin-themed,
spiral notebook
or for odd adults
like my second cousin
who names her chinchillas
after *Harry Potter* villains
and explains Tom Bombadil,
Master of wood, water, and hill,
in detail to any laying claim
to love *Lord of the Rings*.
That immersion
never was for me—

Now, to cradle hope
in my palm—to feel
young again—
is to hide from death.

Final Pages

By: Rachel Bruce

With his children grown, and the jetty finally rotted,
Samwise plants a garden at the base of Mount Doom.

It is slow going.
The soil is vengeful and stubborn,
the air parched.
His steel clashes with vicious ground.
But Sam has battled worse.

Seeking Gorgoroth's native flora,
he finds them sheltering under overhangs
and clustered between pebbles.
They too have felt the crush of evil.
With his hands he guides them to their own leafy scouring.

There is a kind of elegy in the way he rakes the ash,
a devotion in his shovelling.
As he tucks bulbs softly into their beds, his mind wanders;
he hopes the journey West was gentle.

He takes the Red Book with him, of course.
His pages are filled with seed counts and watering schedules
and notes on soil fertility.

Sketches of the garden are richly coloured,
embellished with catalogues of new species.
Doodles of eagles soar around the paper's edges.

He cultivates the earth with care.
Scraping over rock he pictures it —
lush greens blanketing the mountain's side,
the ancient marching usurped by the fluttering of grass.

Sam gives the last of his years to the mountain;
when it is time to come home, they are old friends.

He will not see the majesty of his creation,
but his descendants will marvel at his loving heroism.
I hope you see it one day, overflowing with life:
sweet hops, blushing roses,
and a field of herbs to cure seasickness.

River Anduin, near the Gladden Fields

By: Lauren Suchenski

When I think about the Ring
sitting, festering
in mud and river pebbles
for two and a half millennia,
the odd blade of mottled grass
grazing against it;
I think about fish

their soft fins
catching the side of the band
on any given thursday
in the silence of the sunlit water
I think about waterbugs
tap dancing their tiny feet
across what might have seemed
like a golden bridge
shining against the pale tones
of grooved stones and algae

I think about the wilderness of
thrusting my own hand into any given body of water, never
knowing
what lies in the murk
Yet still, we submerge ourselves any way so often
into the endless flow
of things that move themselves ––

Water, (or molten lava) the gentle
ebb and soft rhythm of movement
whether it be one thousand degrees celsius or seventy degrees
fahrenheit

When I look, with my eyes as wide as they can be, into the tender shade of any given pool I wonder if the water will be a cloak
or a shield; if the connection between
water and lava has been
forged before, and how many times this body
of obscurity
will keep carrying us down stream

Lesser-Known Memoirs of Middle Earth

By: Lynn Hsu

Contributors

Lynn Hsu is a cartoonist and humor writer living in Boston. Her work has been featured in publications such as *Slackjaw, The American Bystander's 251*, and *Little Old Lady Comedy*. She is a member of comedy sketch groups RF News and Glowstick Cocktail. See her funny work at www.lynnihsu.com, and follow her on IG:@loopyline and Twitter:@LynnIHsu.

Scott Cumming never considered himself to be a writer until recently, but turns out he has some stuff to say. He has been published at The Daily Drunk, Punk Noir Magazine, Versification, and Shotgun Honey. His debut poetry chapbook is due for release in December. Host of the Modus Operandi: Flash Fiction podcast and runs Waxing Poetic, a YouTube channel devoted to the best recent poetry from around the net.
Twitter: @tummidge Website: scottcummingwriter.wordpress.com

Melissa Llanes Brownlee (she/her), a native Hawaiian writer, living in Japan, has work published or forthcoming in Booth, Pleiades, The Citron Review, Waxwing, Milk Candy Review, (mac)ro(mic), Necessary Fiction, HAD, The Birdseed, NFFR, trampset, jmww, Superstition Review and Best Small Fictions 2021. Hard Skin, her short story collection, will be coming soon from Juventud Press. She tweets @lumchanmfa and talks story at www.melissallanesbrownlee.com.

Sara Dobbie is a Canadian writer from Southern Ontario. Her work has appeared in places like Sledgehammer Lit, Flash Frog, Ghost Parachute, and elsewhere. Her debut story collection "Flight Instinct" is forthcoming from ELJ Editions (2022). Follow her on Twitter at @sbdobbie and on Instagram at @sbdobwrites.

Donald Carreira Ching (he/him/his) was born and raised in Kahaluʻu, on the island of Oʻahu, Hawaiʻi. His work has appeared in publications such as Rio Grande Review, NonBinary Review, and Every Day Fiction. In 2015, his

54

debut novel, Between Sky and Sea: a Family's Struggle, was published by Bamboo Ridge Press

Matthew Schultz teaches Literature and Creative Writing At Vassar College. Tolkien's essay, "On Fairy-Stories," is a staple in his course on Modernism. You can catch Matt's other work on *Daily Drunk Mag*, in the *Nostalgic AF* Anthology, or in his collection, *Icaros*, forthcoming from ELJ Editions in May 2022.

Arie Kaplan is a comedy writer. His work has been published in *The Daily Drunk*, *MAD Magazine*, *Slate*, *Points in Case*, *Weekly Humorist*, and *National Lampoon*. Arie's television writing credits include *World's Dumbest* (TruTV), *Cyberchase* (PBS Kids), and *Codename: Kids Next Door* (Cartoon Network). He is also the author of numerous books and graphic novels, including *From Krakow to Krypton: Jews and Comic Books*, *The Jurassic Park Little Golden Book*, *The Official Stormtrooper Training Manual*, and *Frankie and the Dragon*. You can find Arie on Twitter @ariekaplan or at www.ariekaplan.com.

Charlie Walsh is a video producer, RPG enthusiast and is tragically allergic to cats. He lives in London with his girlfriend who shares his love for RPGs and cats. Find him on Twitter @AToplad.

Miranda Powers is an actress and writer living in NYC. Check out her latest endeavors at https://mirandapowers.com/

Shiksha Dheda is a writer(?) Sometimes, she dabbles in photography, painting, and baking lopsided layered cakes. Her debut poetry collection, Washed Away, is forthcoming with Alien Buddha Press. She rambles annoyingly on at Twitter: @ShikshaWrites.

Abram Valdez has been there and back again but currently lives in Denton County, Texas. His work has been featured in *HAD, The Daily Drunk, 14*

Hills, Bright Eight, and elsewhere. He used to be a poet, but most of his current work is flash-based and Hobbit-sized.

Rick Hollon (they/them or fey/fem) is a nonbinary intersex queer author, editor, and parent from the American Midwest. Feir work has appeared or is forthcoming in *perhappened, Prismatica, Sledgehammer Lit*, and *Daily Drunk Mag*'s Wickerman anthology. Find them on Twitter at SailorTheia.

Andrew Sippie finds his happy place when writing and reading speculative fiction. He can often be found teaching and tutoring students from all over the world, jogging through the woods, grooving to plunderphonics, and wanting to believe. He's at andrewsippie.com and twitter @AndrewSippie.

Sean D. Zucker is a New York based writer and editor. He currently serves as an editor at The Wildest and is prettier than you expected. More at seanzucker.com or @seanzucker.

Emma Mackenzie is a culture and comedy writer from Oxford, England. She is currently developing a pilot and writes features for magazines. She also provides editing and script consultation services. She can be contacted on Twitter @emmamack01.

Jared Povanda is an internationally published writer and freelance editor from upstate New York. His story, "We Wanted to Sing it From the Light" recently placed first in Versification's Fierce Flash contest. Other work of his can be found in Pidgeonholes, CHEAP POP, and Hobart, among others. Find him @JaredPovanda and jaredpovandawriting.wordpress.com

Kip Knott's most recent full-length collection of poetry, *Clean Coal Burn*, is available from Kelsay Books. His work has appeared or is forthcoming in *Barren, Daily Drunk, Harpy Hybrid Review, HAD, New World Writing,* and *ONE ART*. You can follow him on Twitter at @kip_knott. More of his writing and photography may be accessed at www.kipknott.com.

Tanner Armatis (he/him) has been published by No Contact, the Daily Drunk, the Royal Rose, CP Quarterly, and elsewhere. He was reader at the North American Review. You can find more about him on his website tannerarmatis.com or on Twitter @ok_tanner

Sadie Maskery lives in Scotland by the sea. Her first chapbook, Push, is published by Erbacce Press (erbacce-press.co.uk/sadie-maskery) and she can be found on Twitter as @saccharinequeen

Mike Hickman (@MikeHicWriter) is a writer from York, England. He has written for Off the Rock Productions (stage and audio), including 2018's "Not So Funny Now" about Groucho Marx and Erin Fleming. He has recently been published in EllipsisZine, Dwelling Literary, Bandit Fiction, Nymphs, Flash Fiction Magazine, Brown Bag, and Red Fez. His co-written, completed six-part BBC radio sit com remains frustratingly unproduced but he hopes that mentioning it in every biography increases the chance it might be published one day as a pamphlet.

David Calogero Centorbi is a writer that in the 90's earned an MFA in Creative Writing from the University of Arizona. Now, he is writing and working in Detroit, MI. He is the author of Landscapes of You and Me, (AlienBuddha press.) AFTER FALLING INTO DISARRAY (Daily Drunk Press) He can be found here on Twitter: @DavidCaCentorbi.
Blog: davidcentorbi.blogspot.com

Anna E. Fullmer is a Library Assistant at Cleveland Public Library, slinging story times and songs about the ABCs. She writes songs, poems, and to-do lists. Her work has appeared or is forthcoming in *The Daily Drunk*, *FEED*, *Sledgehammer Lit*, and *Not Deer Magazine*. She offers editorial services for *Versification's THE REJECTS*. Twitter @anna_fullmer

Rachel Bruce is a poet from Hitchin, UK. Her work has appeared in *The Telegraph, Second Chance Lit, Eye Flash Poetry* and *Hencroft Hub, Atrium* and *Briefly Zine*. Find her on Twitter @still_emo.

Lauren Suchenski has a difficult relationship with punctuation. She has been nominated twice for the Pushcart Prize and four times for The Best of the Net. Her chapbook "Full of Ears and Eyes Am I" (2017) is available from Finishing Line Press, and a full-length collection "All You Can Measure" as well as a chapbook "All Atmosphere" (Selcouth Station 2022) are forthcoming. You can find more of her writing on Instagram @lauren_suchenski or on Twitter @laurensuchenski.

Follow us on Twitter!